Art and Music Appreciation Journal for Homeschoolers

Nomad Journals

Art and Music Appreciation Journal for Homeschoolers
Copyright © 2019 by Nomad Journals

Creativity takes courage. -- Henri Matisse

If a composer could say what he had to say in words he would not bother trying to say it in music. - Gustav Mahler

Table of Contents

Peter Breugel the Elder 7

Mozart 11

Gustave Courbet 15

Niccolo Paganini 19

J.M.W. Turner 23

Schumann 27

Titian 31

Wagner & Offenbach 35

Leonardo da Vinci 39

Russian Composers 43

Rembrandt Van Rijn 47

Handel 51

Jan Van Eyck 55

Saint-Saens & Berlioz 59

Sandro Botticelli 63

Bach 67

Casper David Friedrich 71

Listz 75

Vincent Van Gogh 79

Mahler / Brucker 83

Peter Breugel the Elder

Peter Brueghel the Elder was a Flemish painter born between 1525 and 1530. He died in 1569.

Paintings to Study:

Landscape with the Fall of Icarus

Children's Games

Tower of Babel

Landscape with the Parable of the Sower

Hunters in the Snow

Peasant Wedding

Title of the work _Hunters in the snow_

What colors do you see? _Red, blue, green, red, white, black, and grey_

What objects do you see? _Axe, stones, mountains houses, footprints, dogs, people, birds, clouds, ice._

What is happening in the artwork? people are coming home from hunting

Do the objects in the artwork look real? They do not look real to me.

Does anything in the artwork remind you of your own life? I have not been hunting so I cant realate.

What ideas / emotions do you think the artwork expresses? sadness,

How do you think the artist was feeling when they created this artwork? I think he felt disaponted

How does the artwork make you feel? I felt gloomy

Does the artist's work look the same in most of their work? the way he made all the people is simular in the paintings

What would you title this artwork? The fail

Write down more of your thoughts about the artist and the artwork. I notiucred he uses a lot of the same colers schemes.

Most of his paintings have people in them.

Wolfgang Amadeus Mozart

Wolfgang Amadeus Mozart was an Austrian composer who lived from 1756 - 1791.

Compositions to Study:

Concerto for Bassoon and Orchestra in B-flat Major, K191

Concerto for Flute and Harp in C, K299

Piano Sonata No. 11 in A Maj, K331

Piano Concerto 20 in D Min, K466

Symphony 40 in G Min, KV550

Quintet in A Maj for Clarinet, K581

Title of the work _Quintet in a maj for clarinet_

What instruments stand out? _Piano and flute stand out most._

How did the music make you feel? _It made me feel calm._

What did you think about when listening to the music? It took alot of hard work.

If the music were in a movie, what would it be about? a love movie

Have you heard this music before? no, I have not.

What did you like or not like about the music? I like that its calm.

Does the music remind you of anything in your own life? not really.

Did you notice any patterns in the music? a little bit its like bum bum bo

What pictures did you see in your mind as you listened? a ball room.

Would you recommend this music to a friend? yes I would

Write down more of your thoughts about the composer and the music. It was really slow. I didn't like it because of hows slow it was. But other than that I loved it.
Please write what you loved about it ->

I like that it uses a lot
of instruments and its clam.

Gustave Courbet

Gustave Courbet was a French painter who lived between 1819 and 1877. He led the Realism movement in the 19th century.

Paintings to Study:

Stonebreakers

Sleeping Spinner

The Wounded Man

Felsiges Flusstal

The Return of the Deer to the Stream at Plasir Fontaine

The Cliffs of Etretat After the Storm

Title of the work __Wounded man__

What colors do you see? __red, brown, white, peach, rusty brown.__

What objects do you see? __man, sword, tree, jacket.__

What is happening in the artwork? a man is hurt

Do the objects in the artwork look real? yes

Does anything in the artwork remind you of your own life? not really

What ideas / emotions do you think the artwork expresses? sadness

How do you think the artist was feeling when they created this artwork? wide range of emotion

How does the artwork make you feel? scared because he might die

Does the artist's work look the same in most of their work? yes

What would you title this artwork? scar of war.

Write down more of your thoughts about the artist and the artwork. He could have made a gun at his side

Niccolo Paganini

Niccolo Paganini was an Italian violinist and composer who lived from 1782 – 1840.

Compositions to Study:

24 Caprices for Solo Violin Op 1

Violin Concerto No 1 in D Maj, Op 6, MS 21

Violin Concerto No 2 in B Min, Op 7, MS 48

Guitar Quartet No 15 in A Min, MS 42

Tarantella in A Min, Op 33, MS 76

Cantibile D for Violin and Piano, Op 17, MS 109

Title of the work _____

_____

What instruments stand out? _____

_____

How did the music make you feel? _____

_____

What did you think about when listening to the music? _____

_____

If the music were in a movie, what would it be about? _____

_____

Have you heard this music before? _____

_____

What did you like or not like about the music? _____

_____

Does the music remind you of anything in your own life? ___

_____

Did you notice any patterns in the music? _____

_____

What pictures did you see in your mind as you listened? _____

_____

Would you recommend this music to a friend? _____

_____

Write down more of your thoughts about the composer and the music. _____

_____

_____

_____

_____

J.M.W. Turner

Joseph Mallard William Turner was a English watercolorist known for landscapes and turbulent marine paintings.

Paintings to Study:

Fisherman at Sea
Snow Storm: Hannibal and his Army Crossing the Alps
Rome From the Vatican
The Burning of the Houses of Parliament
Fighting Temeraire
Rain, Steam and Speed

Title of the work _____

_____

What colors do you see? _____

_____

What objects do you see? _____

_____

_____

What is happening in the artwork? _____

_____

Do the objects in the artwork look real? _____

_____

Does anything in the artwork remind you of your own life? _

_____

What ideas / emotions do you think the artwork expresses? _

_____

How do you think the artist was feeling when they created this artwork? _____

_____

How does the artwork make you feel? _____

_____

Does the artist's work look the same in most of their work? __

_____

What would you title this artwork? _____

_____

Write down more of your thoughts about the artist and the artwork. _____

_____

_____

_____

_____

Robert Schumann

Robert Schumann was a German composer. He was studying law when he decided to become a pianist.

Compositions to Study:

Carnaval for Piano, Op 9

Scenes from Childhood for Piano, Op 15

An Arabeske or Humoreske, Op 20

Symphony No. 1 in B Flat, Op 38

Liederkreis, Op 39

Symphony No. 2 in C, Op 61

Title of the work _____

_____

What instruments stand out? _____

_____

How did the music make you feel? _____

_____

What did you think about when listening to the music? _____

_____

If the music were in a movie, what would it be about? _____

_____

Have you heard this music before? _____

_____

What did you like or not like about the music? _____

_____

Does the music remind you of anything in your own life? ___

_____

Did you notice any patterns in the music? _____

_____

What pictures did you see in your mind as you listened? _____

_____

Would you recommend this music to a friend? _____

_____

Write down more of your thoughts about the composer and the music. _____

_____

_____

_____

_____

Titian

Titian was an Italian painter during the Renaissance.

Paintings to Study:

The Descent of the Holy Ghost

The Supper at Emmaus

Madonna and Child with St. Catherine and a Rabbit

Portrait of Clarissa Strozzi

Portrait of Emperor Charles V at Muhlberg

The Three Ages of Man

Title of the work _____

_____

What colors do you see? _____

_____

What objects do you see? _____

_____

_____

_____

What is happening in the artwork? _____

_____

Do the objects in the artwork look real? _____

_____

Does anything in the artwork remind you of your own life? _

_____

What ideas / emotions do you think the artwork expresses? _

_____

How do you think the artist was feeling when they created this
artwork? _____

_____

How does the artwork make you feel? _____

_____

Does the artist's work look the same in most of their work? __

_____

What would you title this artwork? _____

_____

Write down more of your thoughts about the artist and the
artwork. _____

_____

_____

_____

_____

Richard Wagner and Jacque Offenbach

Richard Wagner was a German composer known for his operas. Jacque Offenbach was a French-German composer known for his operettas.

Compositions to Study:
Siegfried Idyll

Flight of the Valkyries

The Love Feast of the Twelve Apostles

Galop Infernal from Orpheus in the Underworld (Can-Can)

Selections from the Tales of Hoffmann

Symphony No. 2 in C, Op 61

Title of the work _____

_____

What instruments stand out? _____

_____

How did the music make you feel? _____

_____

What did you think about when listening to the music? _____

_____

If the music were in a movie, what would it be about? _____

_____

Have you heard this music before? _____

_____

What did you like or not like about the music? _____

_____

Does the music remind you of anything in your own life? ___

_____

Did you notice any patterns in the music? _____

_____

What pictures did you see in your mind as you listened? _____

_____

Would you recommend this music to a friend? _____

_____

Write down more of your thoughts about the composer and the music. _____

_____

_____

_____

_____

Leonardo da Vinci

Leonardo da Vinci was a polymath, which means he was interested in a lot of things. He studied art, inventing, architecture, literature, mathematics, geology and more.

Paintings to Study:

Genevra

The Virgin of the Rocks

Lady with Ermine

The Last Supper

Mona Lisa

Self Portrait

Title of the work _____

_____

What colors do you see? _____

_____

What objects do you see? _____

_____

_____

What is happening in the artwork? _____

_____

Do the objects in the artwork look real? _____

_____

Does anything in the artwork remind you of your own life? _

_____

What ideas / emotions do you think the artwork expresses? _

_____

How do you think the artist was feeling when they created this
artwork? _____

_____

How does the artwork make you feel? _____

_____

Does the artist's work look the same in most of their work? __

_____

What would you title this artwork? _____

_____

Write down more of your thoughts about the artist and the
artwork. _____

_____

_____

_____

_____

Nikolai Rimsky-Korsakov and Alexander Borodin

Nikolai Rimsky-Korsakov was a Russian composer.
Alexander Borodin was a Russian chemist and a composer.

Compositions to Study:

Scheherazade

Symphony 2 Antar

Cappriccio Espagnol

Polovtsian Dances

Title of the work _____

_____

What instruments stand out? _____

_____

How did the music make you feel? _____

_____

_____

_____

What did you think about when listening to the music? _____

_____

If the music were in a movie, what would it be about? _____

_____

Have you heard this music before? _____

_____

What did you like or not like about the music? _____

_____

Does the music remind you of anything in your own life? ___

_____

Did you notice any patterns in the music? _____

_____

What pictures did you see in your mind as you listened? _____

_____

Would you recommend this music to a friend? _____

_____

Write down more of your thoughts about the composer and the
music. _____

_____

_____

_____

_____

Rembrandt van Rijn

Rembrandt was a Dutch draftsman, painter and printmaker. He's considered one of the greatest visual artists in history.

Paintings to Study:

The Night Watch

The Raising of the Cross

Shipbuilder Jan Rijcksen and his Wife

Aristotle Contemplating a Bust of Homer

Supper at Emmaus

The Prodigal Son

Title of the work _____

_____

What colors do you see? _____

_____

What objects do you see? _____

_____

_____

_____

What is happening in the artwork? _____

_____

Do the objects in the artwork look real? _____

_____

Does anything in the artwork remind you of your own life? _

_____

What ideas / emotions do you think the artwork expresses? _

_____

How do you think the artist was feeling when they created this
artwork? _____

_____

How does the artwork make you feel? _____

_____

Does the artist's work look the same in most of their work? __

_____

What would you title this artwork? _____

_____

Write down more of your thoughts about the artist and the
artwork. _____

_____

_____

_____

_____

George Frederick Handel

George Frederick Handel was a German born English composer who spent most of his life in London.

Compositions to Study:

Messiah, an oratorio

Water Music

Any Organ Concerto

Rinaldo

Harmonious Blacksmith

Title of the work _____

_____

What instruments stand out? _____

_____

How did the music make you feel? _____

_____

_____

_____

What did you think about when listening to the music? _____

_____

If the music were in a movie, what would it be about? _____

_____

Have you heard this music before? _____

_____

What did you like or not like about the music? _____

_____

Does the music remind you of anything in your own life? ___

_____

Did you notice any patterns in the music? _____

_____

What pictures did you see in your mind as you listened? _____

_____

Would you recommend this music to a friend? _____

_____

Write down more of your thoughts about the composer and the
music. _____

_____

_____

_____

_____

Jan Van Eyck

Jan Van Eyck was a Flemish painter during the Renaissance. He created the oil glazing technique.

Paintings to Study:
Birth of John the Baptist
Madonna with Child Reading
Adoration of the Lamb
The Annunciation
Arnolfini Wedding
Man in a Red Turban

Title of the work _____

_____

What colors do you see? _____

_____

What objects do you see? _____

_____

_____

_____

What is happening in the artwork? _____

_____

Do the objects in the artwork look real? _____

_____

Does anything in the artwork remind you of your own life? _

_____

What ideas / emotions do you think the artwork expresses? _

_____

How do you think the artist was feeling when they created this
artwork? _____

_____

How does the artwork make you feel? _____

_____

Does the artist's work look the same in most of their work? __

_____

What would you title this artwork? _____

_____

Write down more of your thoughts about the artist and the
artwork. _____

_____

_____

_____

_____

Hector Berlioz and Camille Saint-Saenz

Hector Berlioz was a French composer and a conductor in the 19th century. Charles Camille Saint-Saenz also was a 19th century composer remembered for his symphonic poems.

Compositions to Study:

Saint-Saenz: Symphony No 3 in C Min
Saint-Saenz: Danse Macabre
Berlioz: Symphonie Fantastique
Berlioz: Dance of the Sylphs

Title of the work _____

_____

What instruments stand out? _____

_____

How did the music make you feel? _____

_____

_____

What did you think about when listening to the music? _____

_____

If the music were in a movie, what would it be about? _____

_____

Have you heard this music before? _____

_____

What did you like or not like about the music? _____

_____

Does the music remind you of anything in your own life? ___

_____

Did you notice any patterns in the music? _____

_____

What pictures did you see in your mind as you listened? _____

_____

Would you recommend this music to a friend? _____

_____

Write down more of your thoughts about the composer and the
music. _____

_____

_____

_____

_____

Sandro Botticelli

Sandro Botticelli was an esteemed Italian painter during the Renaissance period.

Paintings to Study:

Fortitude

Primavera

Madonna of the Magnificat

The Birth of Venus

A Young Man Being Introduced to the Seven Liberal Arts

Calumny of Apelles

Title of the work _____

_____

What colors do you see? _____

_____

What objects do you see? _____

_____

_____

What is happening in the artwork? _____

_____

Do the objects in the artwork look real? _____

_____

Does anything in the artwork remind you of your own life? _

_____

What ideas / emotions do you think the artwork expresses? _

_____

How do you think the artist was feeling when they created this
artwork? _____

_____

How does the artwork make you feel? _____

_____

Does the artist's work look the same in most of their work? __

_____

What would you title this artwork? _____

_____

Write down more of your thoughts about the artist and the
artwork. _____

_____

_____

_____

Johann Sebastian Bach

Johann Sebastian Bach was a composer and musician of the Baroque period.

Compositions to Study:

Magnificat in D

Chaconne

Brandenberg Concerto No 6

BWV 1, How Lovely Shines the Morning Star – Church Cantata

Title of the work _____

_____

What instruments stand out? _____

_____

How did the music make you feel? _____

_____

_____

What did you think about when listening to the music? _____

_____

If the music were in a movie, what would it be about? _____

_____

Have you heard this music before? _____

_____

What did you like or not like about the music? _____

_____

Does the music remind you of anything in your own life? ___

_____

Did you notice any patterns in the music? _____

_____

What pictures did you see in your mind as you listened? _____

_____

Would you recommend this music to a friend? _____

_____

Write down more of your thoughts about the composer and the
music. _____

_____

_____

_____

_____

Caspar David Friedrich

Caspar David Friedrich was a German landscape painter in the 19th century.

Paintings to Study:

The Cross in the Mountains

The Wanderer Above the Mists

Chalk Cliffs on Rugen

On Board a Sailing Ship

Moon Rising Over the Sea

Woman at a Window

Title of the work _____

_____

What colors do you see? _____

_____

What objects do you see? _____

_____

_____

_____

What is happening in the artwork? _____

_____

Do the objects in the artwork look real? _____

_____

Does anything in the artwork remind you of your own life? _

_____

What ideas / emotions do you think the artwork expresses? _

_____

How do you think the artist was feeling when they created this
artwork? _____

_____

How does the artwork make you feel? _____

_____

Does the artist's work look the same in most of their work? __

_____

What would you title this artwork? _____

_____

Write down more of your thoughts about the artist and the
artwork. _____

_____

_____

_____

Franz Liszt

Franz Liszt was a Hungarian composer, pianist, conductor, music teacher and organist during the Romantic period.

Compositions to Study:

Piano Concerto No 1

Hungarian Rhapsody No 2

Les Preludes

Liebestraum for Piano

Piano Sonata in B Min

Mephisto Waltz

Title of the work _____

_____

What instruments stand out? _____

_____

How did the music make you feel? _____

_____

What did you think about when listening to the music? _____

_____

If the music were in a movie, what would it be about? _____

_____

Have you heard this music before? _____

_____

What did you like or not like about the music? _____

_____

Does the music remind you of anything in your own life? ___

_____

Did you notice any patterns in the music? _____

_____

What pictures did you see in your mind as you listened? _____

_____

Would you recommend this music to a friend? _____

_____

Write down more of your thoughts about the composer and the music. _____

_____

_____

_____

_____

Vincent Van Gogh

Vincent Van Gogh was a Dutch post-impressionist painter. He is one of the most famous artists in history.

Paintings to Study:
The Starry Night
The Chair and the Pipe
The Night Cafe
Self Portrait as an Artist
The Vase with Sunflowers
Bedroom at Aries

Title of the work _____

_____

What colors do you see? _____

_____

What objects do you see? _____

_____

_____

What is happening in the artwork? _____

_____

Do the objects in the artwork look real? _____

_____

Does anything in the artwork remind you of your own life? _

_____

What ideas / emotions do you think the artwork expresses? _

_____

How do you think the artist was feeling when they created this
artwork? _____

_____

How does the artwork make you feel? _____

_____

Does the artist's work look the same in most of their work? __

_____

What would you title this artwork? _____

_____

Write down more of your thoughts about the artist and the
artwork. _____

_____

_____

_____

Anton Bruckner and Gustav Mahler

Anton Bruckner was an Austrian composer and organist.
Gustav Mahler was an Austrian-Jewish composer and
conductor.

Compositions to Study:

Mahler: Symphony No 1
Mahler: Symphony No 9
Mahler: Kindertotenlieder
Bruckner: Symphony No 4

Title of the work _____

_____

What instruments stand out? _____

_____

How did the music make you feel? _____

_____

_____

What did you think about when listening to the music? _____

_____

If the music were in a movie, what would it be about? _____

_____

Have you heard this music before? _____

_____

What did you like or not like about the music? _____

_____

Does the music remind you of anything in your own life? ____

_____

Did you notice any patterns in the music? _____

_____

What pictures did you see in your mind as you listened? _____

_____

Would you recommend this music to a friend? _____

_____

Write down more of your thoughts about the composer and the
music. _____

_____

_____

_____

_____

Made in the USA
Coppell, TX
29 March 2021